Michelangelo Buonarroti , Joseph Fisher, University of Oxford Galleries

Eighty-four Etched Fac-Similes

on a reduced scale, after the original studies by Michael Angelo and Raffaelle in the University Galleries, Oxford. Second Series

Michelangelo Buonarroti , Joseph Fisher, University of Oxford Galleries

Eighty-four Etched Fac-Similes
on a reduced scale, after the original studies by Michael Angelo and Raffaelle in the University Galleries, Oxford. Second Series

ISBN/EAN: 9783337423223

Printed in Europe, USA, Canada, Australia, Japan

Cover: Foto ©Andreas Hilbeck / pixelio.de

More available books at **www.hansebooks.com**

A HOLY FAMILY.

From the collection of M. Buonarroti.

Bequeathed to the University Gallery by G. Fairholme Esq of Greenknowe R——.

EIGHTY-FOUR ETCHED FAC-SIMILES,

ON A REDUCED SCALE,

AFTER THE

ORIGINAL STUDIES

BY

MICHAEL ANGELO AND RAFFAELLE

IN THE

UNIVERSITY GALLERIES, OXFORD.

ETCHED AND PUBLISHED BY

JOSEPH FISHER,

BEAUMONT-STREET.

Second Series.

OXFORD,

M DCCC LXII.

A CATALOGUE OF EIGHTY-FOUR PRINTS

CONTAINED IN THIS SECOND VOLUME.

MICHAEL ANGELO.

A Woman sitting playing with a Child—who stands on her knees;
a Study from life, of which he has made use in the Sistine Chapel. It
is executed in black chalk, washed with bistre of a grey tone. Size
7 in. by 5¼. From the Collection of W. Y. Ottley, Esq.

1. THE Holy Family, painted by Venusti. Bequeathed to the
Galleries by G. Fairholme, Esq.

2. The whole of the composition of the Last Judgment. An
admirable Drawing, highly finished with pen and bistre wash; the
figure of Satan in the boat is of a different tint. 1532.

Size, 22 in. by 16¼. From the Collections of the Casa Buonaroti
and W. Y. Ottley, Esq.

3. Study of several figures for the bottom part of the Last
Judgment. A finished Drawing in red chalk.

Size, 14 in. by 9⅜. From the Collection of R. Cosway, Esq.

4. Death's Head in the Last Judgment. Pen, washed with grey.

5. A most elaborate Drawing—of the subject of the whole of
the Ceiling of the Sistine Chapel. Pen washed with bistre, by
Julio Clovio.

Size, 21¾ in. by 10¼. From the Collection of W. Y. Ottley, Esq.

6. The Crucifixion—a noble Study for our Lord on the Cross,
and two of the Apostles, one on each side. This Design is exe-

cuted in black and white chalk, and has several *Pentimenti's.*
1532—1540.

Size, 11 in. by 9¼. From the Collections of M. Buonaroti and the Chevalier Vicar.

7. A careful **Drawing** of our Saviour **on the Cross—as painted by** *Marcello Venusti.* **Black chalk.**

Size, 14¼ in. by 10. From the Collection of the Chevalier Vicar.

8. The Taking Down from **the Cross. A grand composition of** ten figures, drawn in red chalk.

Size, 10¼ in. by 6¼. From the Collections of J. Hudson, Esq., J. Richardson, Esq.
and Sir J. Reynolds.

9. The Taking Down from the Cross. A very splendid **compo**sition, most important, as no picture is known of this subject. This grand design is of the first order; it is executed in red chalk.

Size, 14¼ in. by 11. **From the** Collection of the Baron de Non.

10. Samson and **Delilah. Drawn in** red chalk ; a superb Drawing. 1510—1512.

Size, 15½ in. by 10¾. **From** the Collections **of the Buonaroti Family**
and the Chev. **Vicar.**

11. Head of a Man—in **a** sort of **Phrygian cap, with his mouth open, as if** singing. The **expression truly surprising; drawn with** red chalk: his **hand holds his cloak together. Evidently from nature,** and highly interesting. from its **extreme finish and truth.**

Size, 6 in. by 5. From the Collection of the Duke of **Modena.**

12. Head of **a** Man—strongly expressive **of malevolence; evi**dently drawn **from** life. Executed in red **chalk, the face** highly finished, and **the cap** and drapery freely sketched.

Size, 11 in. by 8. **From** the Collections of M. Buonaroti, the Chevalier Vicar,
and W. Y. Ottley, **Esq.**

13. A Female **Portrait** in profile—**Victoria** Colonna. Executed in red chalk.

Size, 8¼ in. by 6¼. From the Collections of **M.** Buonaroti and the Chevalier Vicar.

14. A **sheet of** Studies of Hands—also the Body of a Man. **Powerfully drawn,** bistre pen.

Size, 16¼ in. by 10¾. From the Collection of the Chevalier Vicar.

15. A **Female winding** thread, **a** design for one of the Sybils in the Sistine Chapel. 1509.

16. A fine sheet of Studies of **male and female Heads.** In red chalk.

Size, 15¼ in. by 11. From the Collection **of J. Harman,** Esq.

17. Study **of a** Female Head—and **an** *anatomical Study* of a **Leg.** In black **chalk.**

Size, 8¼ in. by 6¼. From the Collections of Sir Peter Lely, Mr. Richardson,
and Sir Joshua Reynolds.

18. Two figures—in large cloaks: one in an attitude of thought; on the reverse is the head of a man in a cap. Executed with the pen and bistre.

19. A Note in the Hand-writing of Michael Angelo.

20. Horses, &c. Very spirited pen Drawing.

21. A sheet of Studies—a male figure, in red chalk; also a hand, smaller figures, and architectural. In bistre pen.

Size, 11¼ in. by 7¾. From the Collections of Mariette and the Marquis Legoy.

22. A Cupid—undraped; probably a Design for the celebrated Statue which he made and buried, to be dug up as an antique, by which he deceived the antiquaries of Rome, and established his reputation. It is highly finished in black chalk; and is, in point of grace and classic feeling, equal to the best of the Greek sculptors.

23. Head of a Cupid—probably a Study for the head of the celebrated Statue which (as before stated) had been taken for antique workmanship. It is in the Greek taste, and executed in red chalk.

Size, 6¼ in. by 5—the other, 8¼ in. by 5¼. From the Collections of M. Buonaroti
and the Chevalier Vicar.

A sheet of Studies of Hands. Powerfully drawn with pen and bistre.

RAFFAELLE.

A graceful Study of a young man playing a guitar.   Pen.
From the Collection of the Marquis Antaldi.

1. STUDY for a St. Catharine.   In black chalk, in his early manner.

Size, 14¼ in. by 11.   From the Collection of the Marquis Antaldi.

2. Studies of small figures of the Holy Family, &c.—and also of a Church for a background.   A pen Drawing, *with the Autograph of Raffaelle.*   1501.

Size, 10¼ in. by 8¾.   From the Collection of the Marquis Antaldi.

3. Study, two Figures — Soldier sitting on his Shield, &c. Drawn on a prepared ground with a metal point.

Size, 12½ in. by 8¾.   From the Collection of the Duke of Alva.

4. Two Young Men, one lying on the ground.   Silver point heightened.

Size, 13 in. by 9¼.   From the Collection of the Duke of Alva.

5. A Group of four Warriors—Study for the celebrated Frescoes in the Library of Sienna.

Size, 9 in. by 8¾.   From the Collection of W. Y. Ottley, Esq.

6. A Youth on his knees, probably intended for St. Stephen. 1506.

Size, 10¼ in. by 7¼.   From the Collection of W. Y. Ottley, Esq.

7. Study of a Soldier in the Resurrection ; also a Study for the Almighty, in the Church of Santa Maria, Porta del Popolo.

8. Landscape, with a view of a City.   Pen.

Size, 9¼ in. by 6½.   From the Collection of Mons. Crozat.

9. A Study of Elephants.   Red chalk.

Size, 12¼ in. by 8½.   From the Collection of the Chevalier Vicar, of Rome.

10. Fighting Figures, probably **intended for** the Rape of Helen. **Pen**.

Size, 16¼ in. by 10.   From the Collection of M. Verstegh.

11. A Storm—Saints Praying in a Boat.   Bistre wash.

Size, 5 in. by 4½.   From the Collections of Mr. Richardson and Sir Joshua Reynolds.

12. Charity—a female and three infants.   This very capital Design is executed in black chalk, at the best time of this illustrious Master—first period.

Size, 12¼ in. by 6.   From the Collections of M. de Rover and M. Revil.

13. Jacob Wrestling with the Angel.   Bistre, heightened **with white**.

Size, 16¼ in. by 5¾.   From the Collection of **the Duke of Alva**.

14 Preparing the Savoury Meats—arched **top, as if intended** for one of the Vatican **Frescoes.   Washed with bistre and height-**ened with white.   1507.

Size, 10¼ in. by 5.   **From the Collection of the Duke of Alva.**

15. Abraham offering up Isaac.   Bistre, heightened with white.

Size, 12¼ in. by 8¾.   From the Collection of the Duke of Modena.

16. Moses striking the Rock—Study for one of the Fresco Paintings in the **Vatican**.   A fine composition, drawn in bistre and heightened with white.

Size, 11¼ in. by 9.   From the Collection of the Chev. Vicar.

17. **The** Salutation of the Virgin.   Grey colour, heightened.

Size, 12¾ in. by 8½.   From the Collection of the Marquis Legoy.

18. The Adoration of the Magi.   Drawn in bistre and height-ened with white.

Size, 12¼ in. by 8½.   From the Collection of J. Harman, Esq.

19. The Adoration of the Kings—the centre portion of the large Tapestry in the Vatican.   In bistre, heightened with white. 1518.

Size, 15¾ in. by 9¾.   From the Collection of R. Udney, Esq.

20. A Holy Family—and Adoration of the Shepherds.   Twelve Figures drawn with the pen.

Size, 15¼ in. by 10¼.   From the Collections of the Chevalier Vicar and W. Y. Ottley, Esq.

21. A Sketch for a picture of the Madonna and Infant Saviour. With the pen.

From the Collection of the Duke of Alva.

22. Virgin and Child. **1503**.

22*. The Virgin seated, with a Book. 1505.

Size, 8½ in. by 5½. From the Collection of the Marquis Antaldi.

23. The Virgin embracing the Infant Saviour. A most graceful and beautiful composition, engraved by Marc **Antonio**.

Size, 6¾ in. by 5½. From the Collection of the Marquis Legoy.

24. Study, in red chalk, for the head **of St. Elisabeth in the** Picture called the Perla, now in Madrid.

Size, 9¾ in. by 7¾. From the Collection of the Chev. Vicar.

25. **Our Lord Crowning the Virgin. 1516.**

Size, 13¾ in. by 11¼. From the Collections of Mariette, M. Bordage, and Lempereur.

26. **The Virgin and the Apostles Mourning over the Body of our Lord.**

Size, 12¾ in. by 9¼. From the Collection of King Charles the First.

27. Study—of three figures for the **celebrated Borghese Picture** representing the Saviour carried to His tomb. **This Study is most** interesting, as proving the care of this illustrious Master **in pre-** paring for his Pictures. The figures in the present **Drawing are** unclothed, to mark the anatomy; the Body of our Lord **is slightly** indicated in red chalk. It is executed with the pen and **bistre.** 1508.

Size, 11¼ in. by 9¼. From the Collections of T. della Vite and the Marquis Antaldi.

28. One of the **Figures, with variations.**

29. Study—called **the Death of** Adonis; evidently a design for the entombment, **reversed.**

30. The miraculous Draught of Fishes. Washed with bistre.

Size, 13½ in. by 6½. From the Collection of the Duke of Alva.

31. A **Female** Figure, in the Vatican Fresco-painting, of Helio-**dorus** driven from the Temple.

32. On the reverse, another Study—Female with Two **Children,** for the Heliodorus. Black chalk.

From the Collection of Sir Joshua Reynolds.

33. Head of the Horse of Heliodorus. This admirable Cartoon **is** inestimable. Mr. Ottley, in the School of Design, thus de-**scribes** it:—"The head of the horse, which was formerly pre-**served in** the Albani Palace at Rome, is of such marvellous per-

fection, that it can only be compared to the finest remains of ancient Greek art."

Size, 27 in. by 21. From the Collections of the Cardinal Albani and W. Y. Ottley, Esq.

34. Female as a Caryatide, Eliodoro.

35. The Resurrection **of** our Saviour. **Washed in bistre, heightened with white.**

Size, 20½ in. **by 12½.** From the Collection of the Chevalier Vicar.

36. **A sheet** of Studies—chiefly for the Picture formerly in the Aldobrandine Palace, late **in** the collection of William Beckford, Esq., and now in the National Gallery. This most admirable Study presents the Head of the St. Catharine, highly finished with the pen, and also **some** Studies of Angels.

37. On the reverse are three several Studies of the St. Catharine, all varying from **the** Painting. It is executed with the pen.

Size, 11 in. by 7. From the Collections of B. West, Esq., P.R.A., and T. Dimsdale, Esq.

38. The upper part of the Fresco-Painting of the Dispute **of the** Sacrament in the Vatican. Thirteen figures, admirably **drawn** with bistre, heightened with white, 1509.

Size, 16 in. by 9½. From the Collections of Mariette, Marquis Legoy, **and T. Dimsdale, Esq.**

39. Study of Heads for ditto.

40. The pretended Miracle **of Bolsena. It is a pen Drawing** in bistre, worked with Indian **Ink.**

Size, **16½** in. by 10½. From the Collection of Sir Joshua Reynolds.

41. The Mount Parnassus—the first Design for this celebrated Fresco **in** the Vatican. Executed with the pen, figures unclothed. **1510.**

Size, 18½ in. by 12. From the Collection of the Chevalier Vicar.

42. Melpomene—a Study for one of the figures in the Fresco of the Vatican; *Mount Parnassus.*

Size, 13½ in. by 10. From the Collection of W. **Y.** Ottley, Esq.

43. Cassandra, or a Muse.

Size, 8½ in. by 5½. **From the Collection of the Marquis Antaldi.**

44. Study for two Sonnets.

45. The suspended Man—endeavouring to escape from **the** fire. A fine model, evidently from the life, for the celebrated Fresco the *Incendio del Borgo* in the Vatican. This splendid Study is executed with **a** bold pencil and bistre, heightened with white.

Size, 16½ in. by 9½. From the Collection of the Baron de Non.

46. The Female carrying two Vases, with Water, in the celebrated Fresco of the *Incendio del Borgo* in the Vatican. Carefully drawn with the pen and bistre, heightened with white; in the manner of M. Angelo.

Size, 15¼ in. by 6¼. From the Collections of Dr. Mead, A. Pond, Esq., and T. Dimsdale, Esq.

47. A Warrior striding over a Fallen Foe. Black chalk.

Size, 15¼ in. by 10¾. From the Collection of M. Dargenville.

48. Samson breaking the jaws of the Lion—a Study with the pen, full of expression, and in surprising preservation.

Size, 10¼ in. by 10¼. From the Collection of Prince Borghese, at Rome.

49. Study of two Heads of the Apostles—in the centre of the Transfiguration. This is one of the finest Drawings existing by this great Master. In black chalk heightened with white.

Size, 19¾ in. by 14¼. From the Collections of M. de Rover of Amsterdam, and J. Harman, Esq.

50. Study of a Foot for one of the figures in the Transfiguration. In black chalk.

51. Study of Figures and Drapery—for St. Michael. Washed in bistre, and heightened with white.

Size, 9¼ in. by 8¼. From the Collection of the Marquis Antaldi.

52. One of the Sibyls—in the celebrated Fresco of the Chiesa della Pace at Rome. A most splendid and elegant figure, executed in red chalk.

Size, 14¼ in. by 7¼. From the Collection of Sir Joshua Reynolds.

53. Seven Persons sitting at Table. Sketched with the metal point, and heightened with white, on a prepared paper; full of expression.

54. Studies of Figures, a Man holding a Book and a Sword, unclothed. A pen Drawing.

55. On the reverse, another Drawing. In the finest time of Raffaelle.

Size, 10¼ in. by 7¼. From the Collection of Mons. Brunet.

56. Studies of four Figures of Warriors. Pen Drawing.

Size, 10¾ in. by 5¾. From the Collection of Mr. Berwick.

57. Three Musicians—a female touching the harp, and two men, one playing a small violin, the other blowing a sort of wind-instrument.

58. Study of a Man—also a Female Head. Pen.

Size, 9¾ in. by 8¼. From the Collection of the Duke of Alva.

From Chambers Hall's Collection.

59. Adoration of the Shepherds. 1505.

60. Presentation in the Temple. A very early pen Drawing. 1504.

61. The Infant Saviour—Bel. Jardinère.

A Saint on his knees—distance, View of a City like Perugia.
From the Collection of the Marquis Antaldi.

THE LAST JUDGEMENT

STUDY OF SEVERAL FIGURES FOR THE BOTTOM PART OF THE LAST JUDGEMENT

Michael Angelo .   W Fisher

Michel Angelo.

TINE CHAPEL.
' Utley. Esq

STUDY FOR THE CRUCIFIXION · OUR LORD ON THE CROSS, AND TWO OF
THE APOSTLES ONE ON EACH SIDE.

OUR SAVIOUR ON THE CROSS.

From the Collection of the Chevalier Vicar

M. Angelo del.
J. Fisher sc.

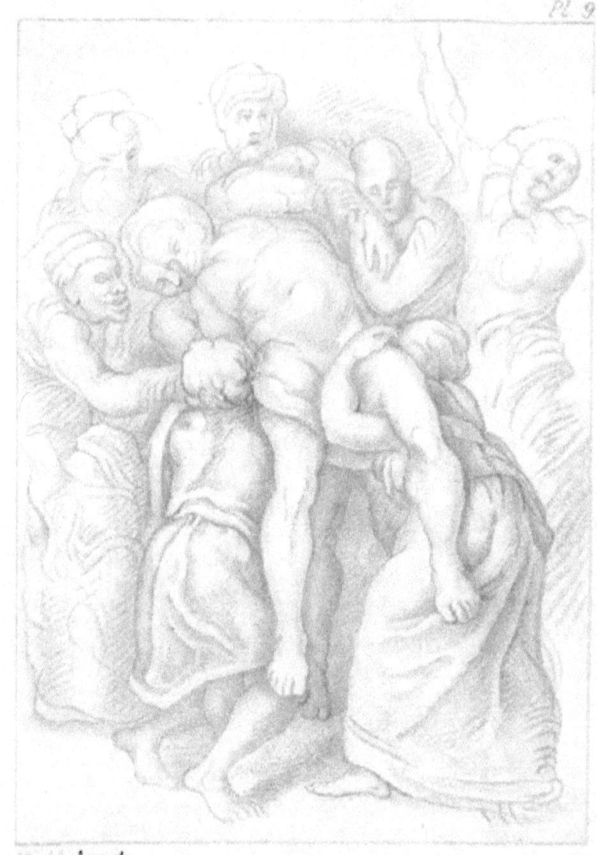

TAKING DOWN FROM THE CROSS.

HEAD OF A MAN·SINGING

21 A MAN EXPRESSIVE OF MALEVOLENCE

A FEMALE PORTRAIT IN PROFILE.

From the Collections of M. Burnarott, and the Chevalier Vicar.

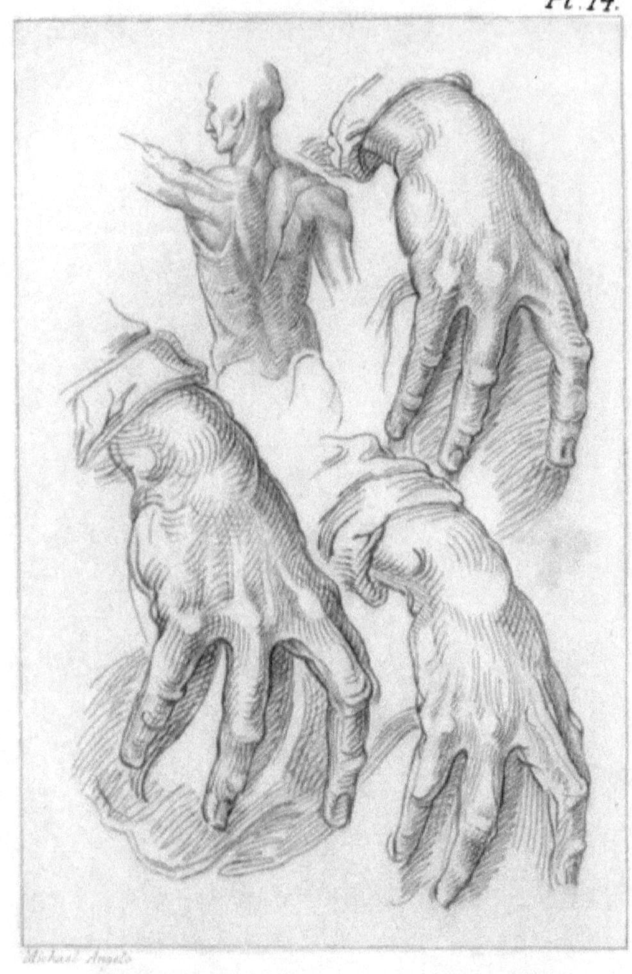

STUDIES OF HANDS AND THE BACK OF A MALE FIGURE.

From the Collection of the Chevalier Vicar.

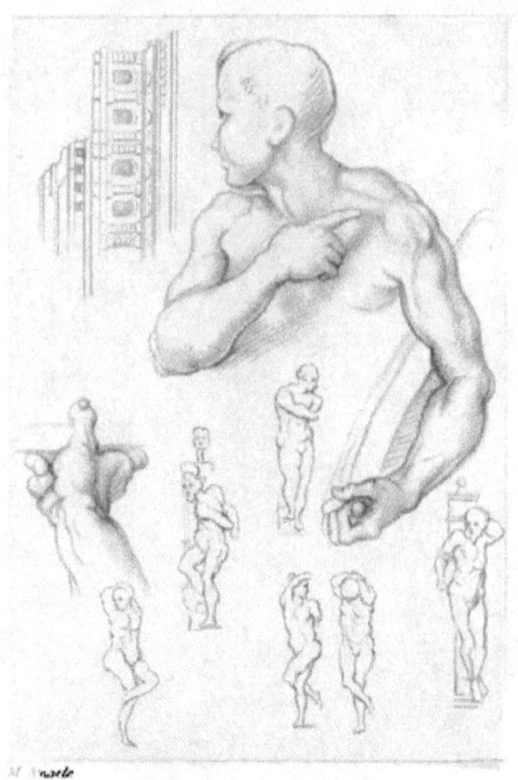

M. Angelo

STUDIES OF MALE AND FEMALE HEADS.

STUDY OF A FEMALE HEAD AND AN ANATOMICAL STUDY OF A LEG.

From the Collection of Sir Patrick M. Richardson and Sir Joshua Reynolds.

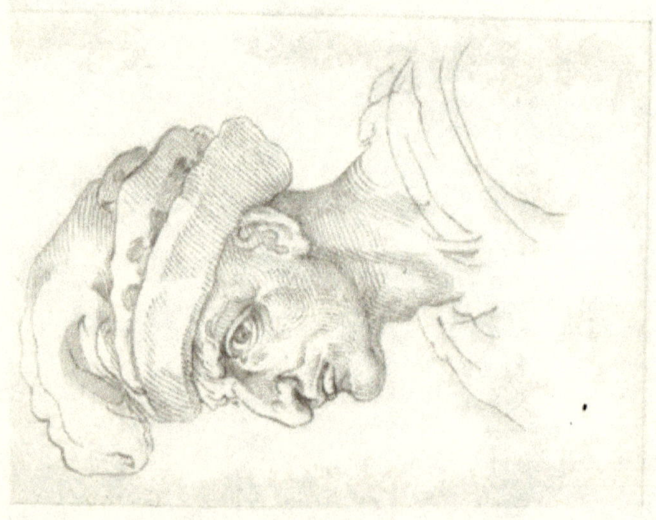

Aueaco mādato chosta p̄ naḡo Sono amẽato homo
te uno Jacto se e dugitacciō e della grosseiza
Sara segniator iquesto lo piglero quādo fia bon
e dibuō filo p̄ c̄ equaossa chosi buono ne agros
chome edecto fate me vo c̄ so sabbi sabato cho
anete poromesso e fareia cosa octima eedana
faro pagare chosta (uats oqua achi mamiṣo

HORSES AND A SMALL STUDY – FIGHTING FOR THE STANDARD

A CUPID UNDRAPED.   HEAD OF A CUPID.

…ORABLY DESIGNS FOR THE CELEBRATED STATUE WHICH HE MADE AND BURIED, TO BE DUG UP AGAIN AS AN ANTIQUE BY WHICH HE DI
…VED THE ANTIQUARIES OF ROME AND ESTABLISHED HIS REPUTATION.

STUDY FOR A SAINT CATHERINE.

From the Collection of the Marquis Antaldi.

Carissimo
Carissimo quanto fracelo

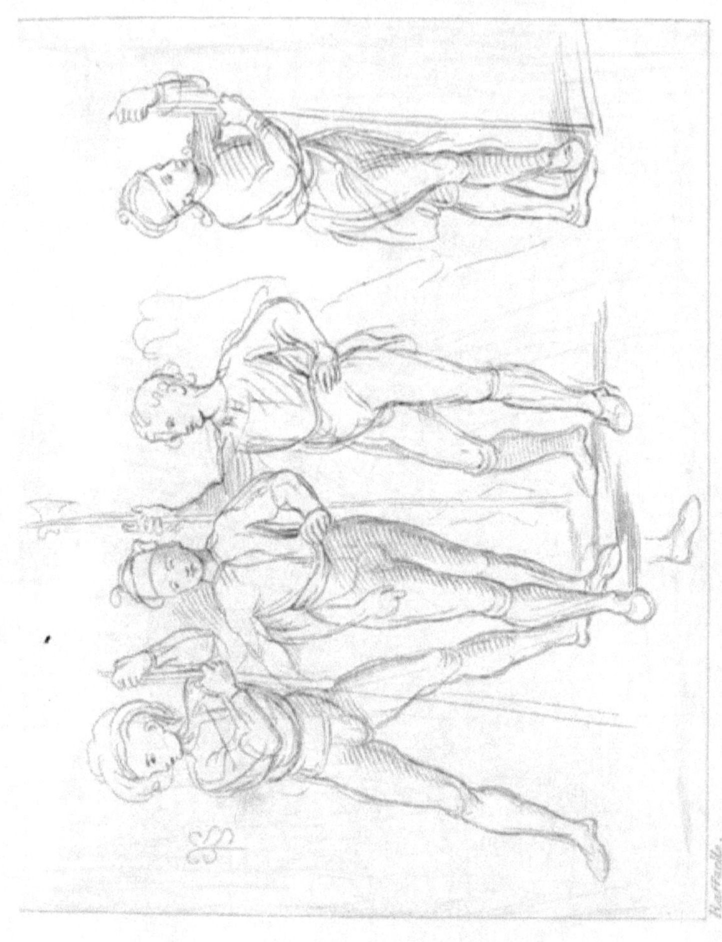

FOUR WARRIORS—FOR PART OF ONE OF THE FRESCOES IN THE LIBRARY AT SIENNA.

A YOUTH ON HIS KNEES PROBABLY INTENDED FOR St STEPHEN.

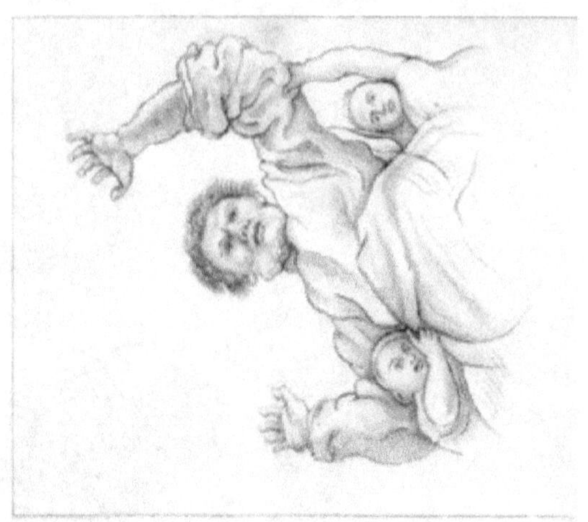

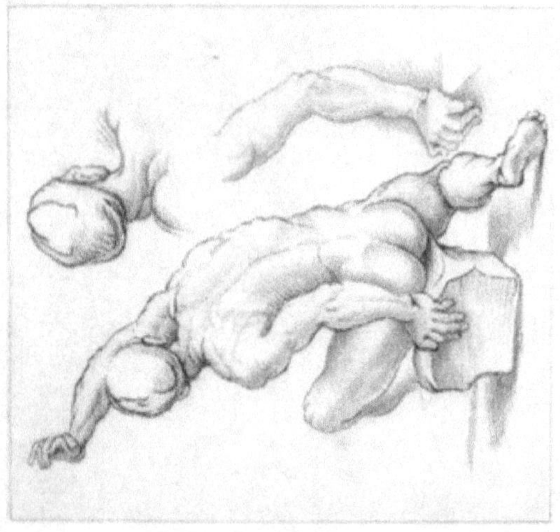

A STUDY OF ELEPHANTS.

PROBABLY A DESIGN FOR WARRIORS IN THE RAPE OF HELEN.

From the Collection of M. Verstolk.

A STORM — SAINTS PRAYING IN A BOAT.

From the Collection of Sir Joshua Reynolds.

CHARITY.

From the Collections of M. de Rover and M. Revil.

JACOB WRESTLING WITH THE ANGEL

From the Collection of the Duke of Alva.

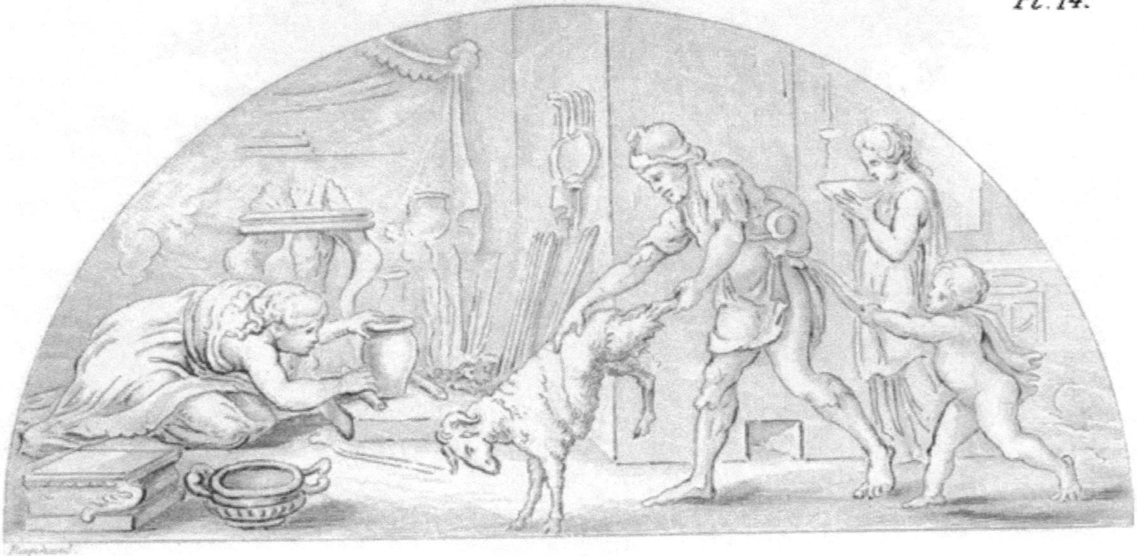

PREPARING THE SAVOURY MEATS.

From the Collection of the Duke of Alva.

ABRAHAMS SACRIFICE.

From the Collection of the Duke of Modena

MOSES STRIKING THE ROCK.

From the Collection of the Chevalier Vicar

THE ANNUNCIATION

From the Collection of the Marquis Antaldi

THE ADORATION OF THE MAGI.

From the Collection of R. Udney Esq.

THE ADORATION OF THE MAGI.

From the Collection of J. Harman, Esq.

A HOLY FAMILY AND ADORATION OF THE SHEPHERDS.

From the Collections of the Chevalier Vicar and W.Y. Ottley Esq.

SKETCH FOR A PICTURE OF THE MADONNA AND INFANT SAVIOUR.
From the Collection of the Duke of Alva.

Raphael. 1507.

THE VIRGIN SEATED STUDYING A BOOK, WITH THE INFANT SAVIOUR.

THE VIRGIN EMBRACING THE INFANT SAVIOUR.

From the Collection of the Marquis Legoy.

STUDY FOR THE HEAD OF S⁺ ELIZABETH IN THE PICTURE CALLED THE M

OUR LORD CROWNING THE VIRGIN.

From the Collection of Mariette

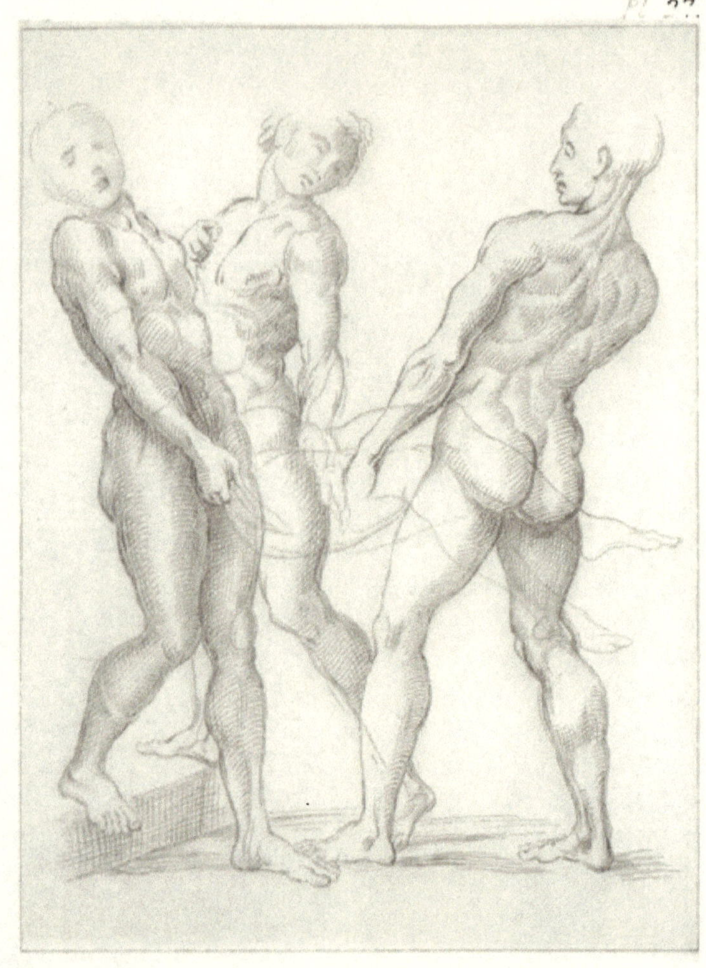

STUDY OF THREE FIGURES FOR THE BORGHESE PICTURE.

OF THE ENTOMBMENT.

From the Collections of Tim della Vite, and the Marquis Antaldi

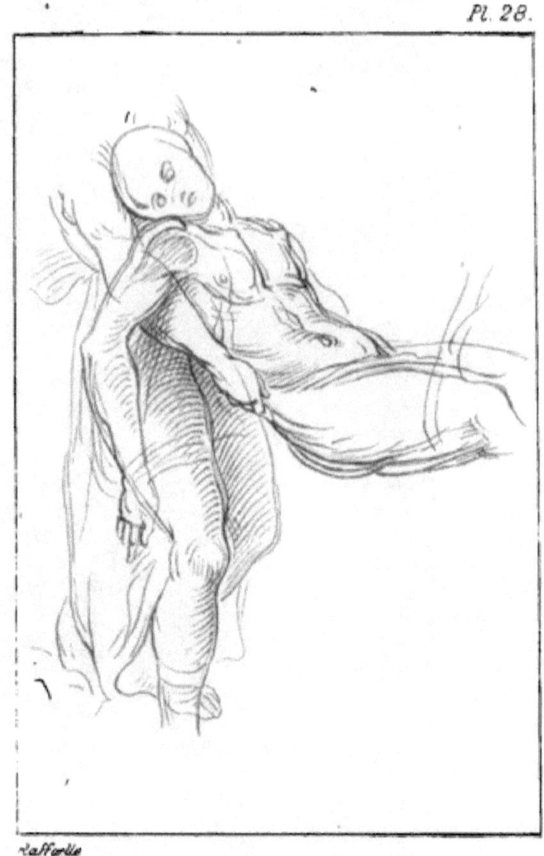

SKETCH FOR THE ENTOMBMENT.

THE MIRACULOUS DRAUGHT OF FISHES.

Raffaelle.

STUDY OF A FEMALE IN THE FRESCO OF HELIODORUS DRIVEN OUT OF THE TEMPL

Raffaelle

HEAD OF THE HORSE. — HELIODORUS.

A CARIATIDE — PAINTED IN CAMAIEU IN THE HALL OF HELIODORUS

From the Collection of Lord Spencer.

Raffaelle.

THE RESURRECTION.

From the Collection of the Chevalier Vicar.

STUDY FOR THE HEAD OF S.t CATHERINE (OF ALEXANDRIA) A PICTURE NOW IN THE NATIONAL GALLERY. PURCHASED OF M.r BECKFORD FOR £3500.

From the Collection of B West Esq P.R.A.

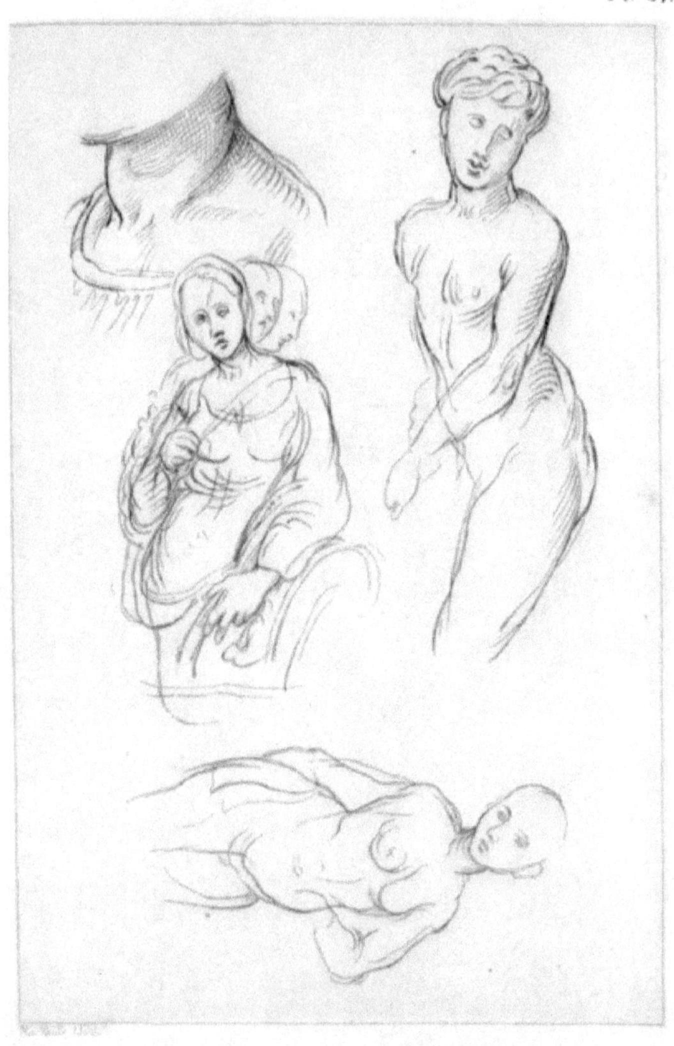

VARIOUS STUDIES FOR THE S.T CATHERINE.

THE UPPER PART OF THE FRESCO PAINTING OF THE DISPUTE ON THE SACRAMENT.

From the Collections of Mariette, Marquis Legoy and T. Dimsdale Esq.

STUDY OF HEADS FOR THE DISPUTE ON THE SACRAMENT.

From the Collection of the Marquis Antaldi.

THE PRETENDED MIRACLE OF BOLSENA.

Pl. 41.
THE MOUNT PARNASSUS.
From the Collection of the Chevalier Vicar

Raffaelle

CASSANDRA, OR A MUSE

From the Collection of the Marquis Antaldi

como nõ podde dir dancona dei
paul quan como disceso fu del celb
casi elmio cor duno amoroso nebo
owicogerro tuti ipenser mei
Pero quanto chio meddi equanto Jo fu
pel gaudio Inccio che nelgeno celo
ma prima campero nel fronto elpelo
che mai lobligo nolga in pensir rei

amor cu men nesscalli cõ doi luce
le doi beh ochi donio meblrago esfacb
la bianca nene edarose nmace
da bei parlar ede unneno cobremi
Forl che tomeo ardo olg nemar nefumi
spegmar potriam quelfocho nens inpiaor
gorchel mio ardor tanto diben miface
cardendo pin dalomor pin dardor mecor

THE SUSPENDED MAN   INCENDIO DEL BORGO

FOR   THE FEMALE CARRYING TWO VASES

...E CELEBRATED FRESCO OF THE *INCENDIO DEL BORG...*

Collections of D.ʳ Mead, A. Pond Esq.ʳ and T. Dimsdale Esq.ʳ

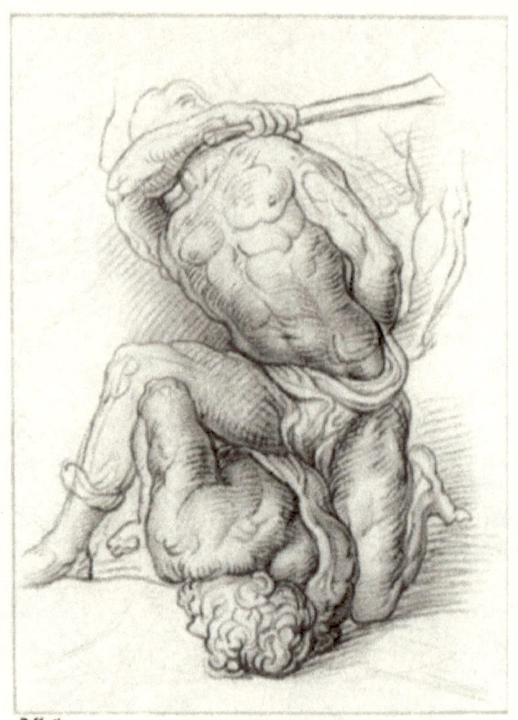

A WARRIOR STRIDING OVER A FALLEN FOE.

From the Collection of M. Duramville.

Raffaelle.

SAMSON BREAKING THE JAWS OF THE LION.

From the Collection of Prince Bonaparte at Rome.

TWO HEADS OF THE APOSTLES IN THE CENTRE OF THE TRANSFIGURATION

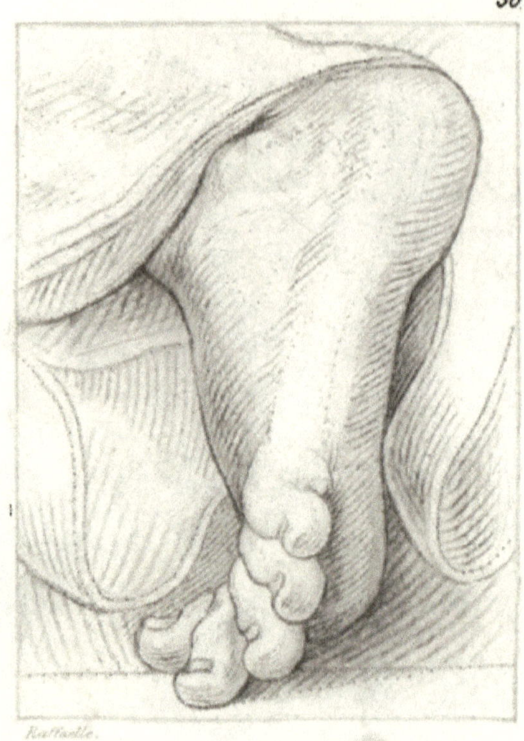

STUDY of A FOOT for one of the figures in the TRANSFIGURATION.

From the Collection of the Chevalier Vicar

STUDY OF FIGURES AND DRAPERY FOR S? MICHAEL.

From the Collection of the Marquis Antaldi.

A SIBYL. *Fresco in the Chiesa della Pace - Rome.*

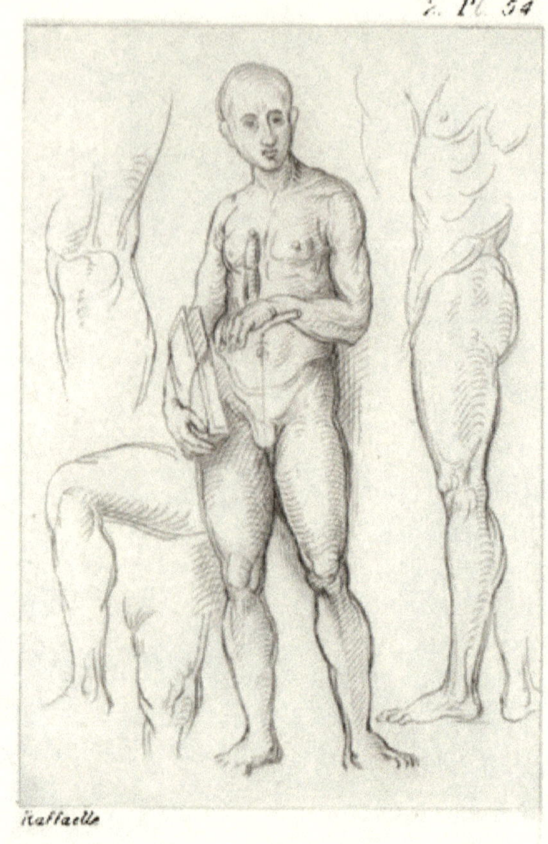

STUDIES—A MAN HOLDING A BOOK AND SWORD.

ON THE REVERSE OF THE LAST PLATE.

FOUR WARRIORS.

From the Collection of M.ʳ Berwick.

Raffaelle.

STUDY OF A MAN --- ALSO A FEMALE HEAD.

Pl. 5.
Fisher
Raffaelle.

THE PRESENTATION IN THE TEMPLE.

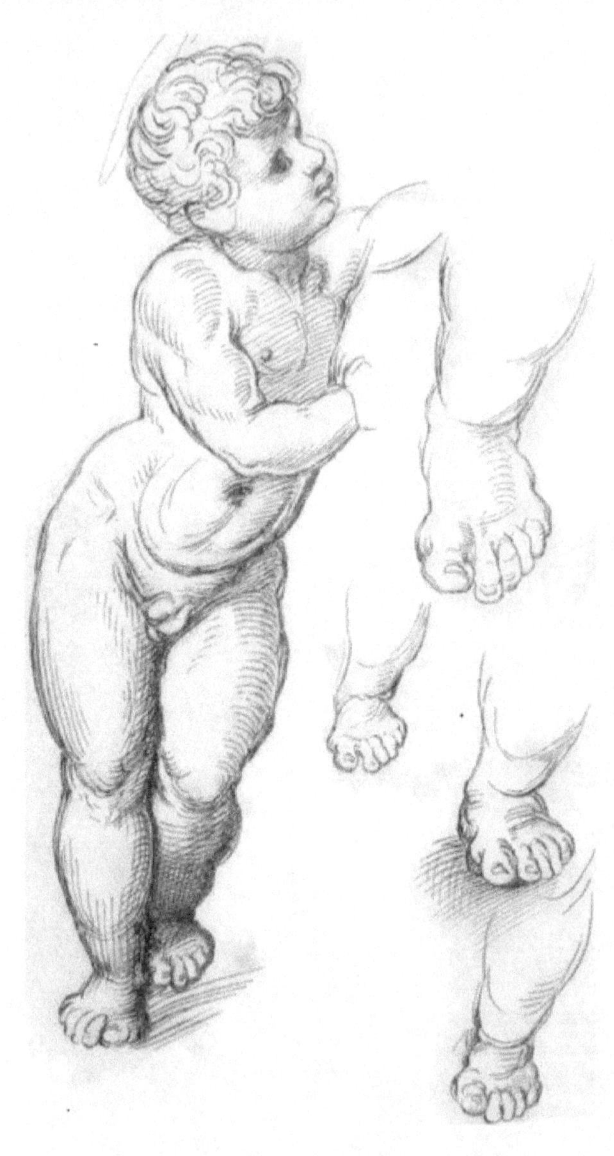